John Christian Bullitt

A review of Mr. Binney's pamphlet on

John Christian Bullitt

A review of Mr. Binney's pamphlet on

ISBN/EAN: 9783337102197

Printed in Europe, USA, Canada, Australia, Japan

Cover: Foto ©Andreas Hilbeck / pixelio.de

More available books at **www.hansebooks.com**

A REVIEW

OF

MR. BINNEY'S PAMPHLET

ON

"THE PRIVILEGE

OF THE

WRIT OF HABEAS CORPUS

UNDER

THE CONSTITUTION."

BY J. C. BULLITT.

PHILADELPHIA:
JOHN CAMPBELL, PUBLISHER,
419 CHESTNUT STREET.
1862.

INTRODUCTION.

In submitting the following remarks to the consideration of such persons as may take the trouble to read them, I solicit the indulgence of a few words of a personal character.

When Mr. Binney's pamphlet on the "Habeas Corpus" made its appearance, I read it with the utmost care and with an earnest endeavor to divest myself of all educational bias. Its propositions were examined as questions of law, and, as far as possible, independently of the influence of preconceived opinions. The result arrived at was a conviction on my mind that in many respects his premises were not well taken, and that his inferences or conclusions were erroneous.

In common with many other persons, as it now appears, I commenced the preparation of a review of his argument. During the period which has since elapsed several such articles have been published. The danger of producing a surfeit of Habeas Corpus pamphlets would have deterred me from adding one more to that number but for the fact that, upon examining these publications, it appeared they all viewed the matter from more or less varying stand-points, and mine differed somewhat from all of them.

I have sought to treat the subject simply and purely in its legal aspects. If the following remarks shall in any degree aid in eliminating the truth, that will be ample compensation for the time and labor bestowed upon them. I ask of those who may read them a candid and impartial consideration of the arguments and authorities presented. Whether they possess any other merit or not, thus much at least is claimed for them : they have been attentively considered and carefully prepared. They are put forth with a sincere desire to promote the cause of truth and the preservation of rights which I, in common with all American citizens, have been taught to cherish as the most sacred of those inherited from our ancestors.

Abstaining from reflections upon the occurrences of the day, my purpose has been simply to present the great constitutional question involved in its true light. It is for the reader to determine with what success this effort has been attended.

JOHN C. BULLITT.

PHILADELPHIA, March 10, 1862.

REVIEW.

THE first three articles of the Constitution of the United States treat of the three departments of the Government respectively: 1. The Legislative; 2. The Executive; 3. The Judiciary.

With a view to facilitate the discussion as to the subject of the Habeas Corpus, to which the following remarks are addressed, such portions of the Constitution as are necessary for reference will be given. They are:

ARTICLE I.

SECTION 1. All legislative powers herein granted shall be vested in a Congress of the United States, which shall consist of a Senate and House of Representatives. . . . . . .

SECTION 8. The Congress shall have power. . . . . .

To declare war, grant letters of marque and reprisal, and make rules concerning captures on land and water.

To raise and support armies; but no appropriation of money to that use shall be for a longer term than two years.

To provide and maintain a navy.

To make rules for the government and regulation of the land and naval forces.

To provide for calling forth the militia to execute the laws of the Union, suppress insurrections, and repel invasions.

To provide for organizing, arming, and disciplining the militia, and for governing such part of them as may be employed in the service of the United States. . . . .

And to make all laws which shall be necessary and proper for carrying into execution the foregoing powers and all other powers vested by this Constitution in the government of the United States, or in any department or officer thereof.

SECTION 9. The migration or importation of such persons as any of the states now existing shall think proper to admit, shall not be prohibited by the Congress prior to the year one thousand eight hundred and eight; but a tax or duty may be imposed on such importation not exceeding ten dollars for each person.

The privilege of the writ of Habeas Corpus shall not be suspended, unless when, in cases of rebellion or invasion, the public safety may require it.

No bill of attainder or *ex post facto* law shall be passed.

AMENDMENTS. ARTICLE III.

No soldier shall, in time of peace, be quartered in any house without the consent of the owner; nor in time of war, but in a manner to be prescribed by law.

ARTICLE IV.

The right of the people to be secure in their persons, houses, papers, and effects, against unreasonable searches and seizures, shall not be violated; and no warrants shall issue but upon probable cause, supported by oath or affirmation, and particularly describing the place to be searched, and the persons or things to be seized.

ARTICLE V.

No person shall be held to answer for a capital, or otherwise infamous crime, unless on a presentment or indictment of a grand jury, except in cases arising in the land or naval forces, or in the militia, when in actual service in time of war or public danger; . . . . . . nor be deprived of life, liberty, or property, without due process of law. . . . .

ARTICLE VI.

In all criminal prosecutions the accused shall enjoy the right to a speedy and public trial by an impartial jury of the State and district wherein the crime shall have been committed, which district shall have been previously ascertained by law, and to be informed of the nature and cause of the accusation. . . .

It will thus be seen that the framers of the Constitution made very ample provision for enabling Congress to pass all laws which any possible contingency arising either from foreign or domestic disturbances could render necessary for the welfare of the country. But it is also apparent that they guarded with the most sedulous care the rights of the people against the exercise of arbitrary or unregulated power.

The suspension of the Habeas Corpus by the Executive department without the authority of an act of Congress has given rise, during the last few months, to much discussion. Among the publications upon this subject that which has perhaps attracted most attention in this community is a pamphlet by Horace Binney, Esq., entitled, "The Privilege of the Writ of Habeas Corpus under the Constitution." It is an elaborate effort to show that the power of suspension belongs, under the Constitution, to the President without, and exclusive of, any control or authority by Congress.

The subject is one of vital importance to the whole people; and such a publication as that of Mr. Binney should not pass down in the constitutional history of the country without comment. If founded in error, it is fraught with most serious mischief; if in truth, discussion will only serve to bring out its verification in bolder relief.

In construing constitutional or legislative enactments, certain rules of interpretation have been adopted by which the meaning of the framers of the instrument or law is to be ascertained. The first of these is the plain rendering of the language used according to the meaning of the words as understood at the time of their adoption. If for any reason, however, there is any ambiguity in the language, then resort must be had to other aids in arriving at the proper construction. Among these are the context, analogy, the object had in view by the framers, their contemporaneous expressions, legislative or judicial interpretation, the opinions of statesmen, jurists and text-writers on the subject; and in fact everything, whether it be historical, juridical or legislative, which can shed any light upon the subject.

Applying the first rule stated above, it would seem hardly to admit of a doubt that the Constitution reposed in Congress alone the power to suspend the privilege of the Writ of Habeas Corpus. But the pamphlet under consideration endeavors, by a process of reasoning of extreme refinement, to establish, not only a denial of the power to Congress, but the vesting it in the President. It is proposed to examine the grounds upon which this doctrine rests.

IS THE CLAUSE A GRANT OF POWER, OR A RESTRICTION?

The first proposition of the pamphlet is, that the Habeas Corpus clause is a grant of the power of suspension. The language used is as follows:

"'The clause in the Constitution of the United States, in regard to the privilege of the Writ of Habeas Corpus, is this:

"'The privilege of the Writ of Habeas Corpus shall not be suspended, unless, when in cases of rebellion or invasion, the public safety may require it.'

The sentence is elliptical. When the ellipsis is supplied it reads thus:

"The privilege of the Writ of Habeas Corpus shall not be suspended, unless, when in cases of rebellion or invasion, the public safety may require it; *and then it may be suspended.*

"This is the necessary effect of the conjunction 'unless,' which reverses the action of the preceding verb; and it will be of perfectly equivalent import and effect if the clause be transposed as follows: 'The privilege of the Writ of Habeas Corpus may be suspended in cases of rebellion or invasion, when the public safety may require it; and it shall not be suspended in any other case.'" (Pamphlet, p. 9.*)

This assumes that there was no pre-existing power to suspend, or rather, that without this clause no authority for its exercise would have been implied from any source, and that the grant of the power is to be found in these words only.

The Constitution provides that a thing shall not be done except under certain contingencies. This would imply that the general power was granted elsewhere, and, but for the clause of restriction, it could have been exercised in all cases to which the general principle would apply.

But the argument inverts the natural construction, and con-

* The references to the pamphlet of Mr. Binney are to the pages of the edition issued by C. Sherman & Son.

verts a restriction into a grant with a qualification. It is true
that this rule may be, and sometimes is adopted by courts in
the construction of statutes, in order to effectuate the intentions
of the Legislature; but it is regarded as an artificial, rather
than a natural mode of construction. The natural construction,
and the constitutional one, too, would seem to be that this was
merely a restriction or limitation of the power already existing,
or conferred by some other portion of the Constitution upon the
department to which the restriction was applied, to wit, the
legislative,—that in all such cases, as the privilege of the Writ
could have been suspended but for this restriction or limitation,
it may still be suspended during the prevalence of rebellion or
invasion, when the public safety may require it. Yet, under
these circumstances, it can only be done by the same department which would have had the power if the restriction had not
been adopted.

It may be asked, whether the power to suspend is conferred
upon Congress, and, if so, where the authority for it is to be
found? Does it exist independently of the Constitution? The
answer is that it does not, as Congress has no powers except
such as are given by the Constitution.

One construction places its derivation under the express grant
of the power to Congress to regulate the courts. This was the
view entertained by Governor Randolph, who was a member of
the Federal Convention that framed the Constitution, and also of
the Virginia Convention which ratified it. In a speech in favor of
its ratification, he uses this language: "But the insertion of the
"negative *restrictions* has given cause of triumph to gentlemen.
"They suppose that it demonstrates that Congress are to have
"powers by implication. I will meet them on that ground. I
"persuade myself that every exception here mentioned is an ex-
"ception, not from general powers, but from the particular powers
"therein vested. To what power in the General Government
"is the exception made respecting the importation of negroes?
"Not from a general power, but from a particular power
"expressly enumerated. This is an exception from the power
"given them of regulating commerce. He asks where is the
"power to which the prohibition of suspending the *Habeas*
"*Corpus* is an exception? I contend that, by virtue of the

"power given to Congress to regulate courts, they could sus-
"pend the Writ of *Habeas Corpus.* This is, therefore, an
"exception to that power." (Elliott's Debates, Vol. III, p. 464.)

It is to be observed, that the Constitution only confers upon
Congress the power to regulate the Federal courts. Therefore,
if the authority to suspend a Writ is derived from that grant, it
must be limited in its application to those particular tribunals.
Hence, it would follow, that the power of suspension, conferred
by the Constitution, would be restricted to the privilege of the
Writ of Habeas Corpus, as enjoyed under the jurisdiction and
practice of the Federal courts alone.

The State courts, not being subject to regulation by Congress,
would be excluded from the operation of the power of suspension. The judges of the latter, however, can issue the Writ of
Habeas Corpus with the same force and effect as those who pre-
side in the courts of the United States. Therefore, if the views
of Governor Randolph are correct, it results that the power of
suspension granted to Congress being limited to the Writs issued
or to be issued by the Federal courts, and having no application
to the State courts, the attempt to suspend the privilege could
and probably would be rendered nugatory by the action of the
latter. Such a glaring defect cannot well be imputed to the
Constitution, and while the opinion of Governor Randolph is
entitled to as much weight as that perhaps of any one who has
ever expounded that instrument, it is contended that in this
instance he has fallen into an error as to the clause under which
the power of suspension is granted. His remarks, however,
contain two propositions which render them worthy of much
consideration in treating this subject: 1. He distinctly avers
that the Habeas Corpus clause is a restriction upon power
granted elsewhere, and is not in itself a grant of any power. 2.
He as decidedly declares that the power of suspension is vested
in Congress.

A different interpretation, and, with all due respect for the
opinions of Governor Randolph, it is suggested, as being a much
more reasonable one, is this: that the authority to suspend the
Habeas Corpus is conferred under the power to provide for the
suppression of insurrection and the repelling of invasion. This
inference is supported by English analogy. The power of sus-

pension was usually exercised under these circumstances by Parliament. It springs from the necessity recognized as existing for the suspension under these circumstances; and finally, the Habeas Corpus clause implies its grant under the power referred to, by providing that it shall not be suspended, unless when, in cases of rebellion or invasion, the public safety may require it.

The power to provide for the suppression of insurrection or invasion is given to Congress. The, Constitution restricts the authority to suspend to such occasions, and the inference is natural that the department charged with the duty of providing for suppression was the one authorized to wield this power for the purpose of attaining the proposed end. The necessity for its exercise upon such occasions renders it one of the means to be employed, and brings it within the provisions contemplated by that clause. The authority to suspend is first given as a means of suppressing insurrection or repelling invasion; and the restriction is then put upon this authority that it shall not be exercised even under those conditions, except when "the public safety may require it."

"Suspension," "insurrection," "invasion," are inseparably bound together. Construe the Constitution in this way and its reading is simple, consistent, and natural.

If, then, it is an error to construe the Habeas Corpus clause as a grant of power, instead of a restriction, all the rest of the argument which is founded upon this error must fall when it is removed. There might be some reason for asserting that it was affirmative rather than restrictive, if there was no other clause in the Constitution under which the grant of the power of suspension would be properly implied.

This interpretation places the power in the Legislative department and in that only, and if adopted is a complete bar to any such claim on the part of the Executive department. Whether correct or not, it is left for the reader to determine, with this suggestion, however, that in order to understand the true meaning of any one clause of the Constitution the whole must be carefully examined and each part read by the light of every other.

THE HISTORY OF THE CLAUSE.

But the history of the clause is relied upon as sustaining the view that it was intended as a grant of power to the Executive department.

After giving that history, the pamphlet remarks: "Enough, "however, is recorded to show that it must have been in the "minds of the delegates under at least three aspects: 1. Sus-"pension of the privilege, and not of the Writ or Act. 2. Sus-"pension by the Legislature, and only by the Legislature. 3. "Suspension generally, and by the department that would be "intrusted in rebellion or invasion with the safety of the public." This is most ingeniously put, and it is followed by the effort to show that the department so intrusted is the Executive, and therefore the power of suspension falls to that department. It is believed that this history does not show that the delegates had in their minds a suspension of the privilege as distinct from that of the Writ; on the contrary, that they regarded *the suspension of the privilege of the Writ* as the generic term including *the suspension of the Writ,* whether as derived from the common law or from any legislative act. It does show that they contemplated its suspension by the Legislature under certain contingencies, but it in no wise countenances the idea that they contemplated conferring the power to suspend upon any other than the Legislative department.

The Convention met in May, 1787, in Philadelphia. On the 29th of May, Mr. Charles Pinckney, of South Carolina, laid before the House a draft of a plan of a Federal Constitution, the VIth Article of which provided, "The Legislature of the "United States shall pass no law on the subject of religion, nor "touching or abridging the liberty of the press; nor shall the "privilege of the Writ of Habeas Corpus ever be suspended, "except in the case of rebellion or invasion."

On the 6th of August the Committee of Detail, consisting of Rutledge, Randolph, Gorham, Ellsworth, and Wilson, reported a draft of a Constitution, but it contained no provision on the subject of the Writ of Habeas Corpus.

On the 20th of August Mr. Pinckney submitted to the House,

in order to be referred to the Committee of Detail, the following proposition, among others : " The privileges and benefits of the " Writ of Habeas Corpus shall be enjoyed in this Government in " the most expeditious and ample manner, and shall not be sus- " pended by the Legislature, except upon the most urgent and " pressing occasions, and for a limited time not exceeding —— " months."

On the 28th of the same month, "Mr. Pinckney, urging the " propriety of securing the benefit of the Habeas Corpus in the " most ample manner, moved that it should not be suspended " but on the most urgent occasions, and then only for a limited " time, not exceeding twelve months."

" Mr. Rutledge was for declaring the Habeas Corpus invio- "late. He did not conceive that a suspension could ever be "necessary at the same time through all the States."

"Mr. Gouverneur Morris moved that the privilege of the " Writ of Habeas Corpus should not be suspended, unless when, "in cases of rebellion or invasion, the public safety may "require it."

"Mr. Wilson doubted whether in any case a suspension could "be necessary, as the discretion now exists with judges in most "important cases to keep in gaol, or admit to bail."

"The first part of Mr. Gouverneur Morris's motion, to the "word 'unless,' was agreed to nem. con. On the remaining part "the vote stood: Aye—New Hampshire, Massachusetts, Con- "necticut, Pennsylvania, Delaware, Maryland and Virginia—7. "Nay—North Carolina, South Carolina, Georgia—3." (Elliott's Debates, Vol. V, pp. 131, 376, 445, 484.)

It will be perceived, by a reference to the above, that the delegates spoke of "the privilege of the Writ of Habeas Cor- "pus," "the privileges and benefits of the Writ of Habeas "Corpus," and "the Habeas Corpus," indifferently, as con- veying the same general meaning.

We find in the letter of Luther Martin, one of the ablest and most enlightened lawyers of his day, to the Speaker of the House of Delegates of Maryland, of January 27, 1788, assigning his reasons for voting in the negative upon this clause, that he speaks of suspending the Habeas Corpus Act. He says: " By "the next paragraph, the General Government is to have a "power of suspending the Habeas Corpus Act in cases of "rebellion or invasion. As the State Governments have a "power of suspending the Habeas Corpus Act in those cases, "it was said there could be no reason for giving such a power "to the General Government, since, whenever the state which "is invaded, or in which an insurrection takes place, finds its "safety requires it, it will make use of that power; and it was "urged, that if we give this power to the General Government, "it would be an engine of oppression in its hands, since, when-"ever a state should oppose its views, however arbitrary and "unconstitutional, and refuse submission to them, the General "Government may declare it an act of rebellion; and, sus-"pending the Habeas Corpus Act, may seize upon the persons "of those advocates of freedom who have had virtue and reso-"lution enough to excite the opposition, and may imprison "them during its pleasure in the remotest parts of the Union; "so that a citizen of Georgia might be Bastiled in the farthest "part of New Hampshire, or a citizen of New Hampshire in "the farthest extreme of the South—cut off from their family, "their friends, and their every connection.

"These considerations induced me, sir, to give my negative "also to this clause." (Elliott's Debates, Vol. I, p. 375.)

The error of Mr. Martin, in speaking of the Habeas Corpus Act, taken in connection with the language used in the Convention, indicates clearly that the delegates had in their minds the general proposition of the suspension of the Habeas Corpus, and that the words, as finally used, were adopted, as expressing most appropriately the general idea that the privilege or benefit of the Writ should not be suspended. The words of the clause were generic, embracing the suspension of the privilege of the Writ, whether the Writ itself was authorized by the common law or by legislation. This language also makes it apparent that the delegates did not contemplate its suspension by any other than the Legislative department.

The clause, as found in Mr. Pinckney's draft of the 29th of May, is the latter part of a clause restricting the power of the Legislature as to the subject of religion and the liberty of the press, and it is but reasonable to infer that the latter part of the sentence relates back to the first, and operates as a restriction upon the same department which was embraced by the preceding restrictive provisions.

If there was any doubt about this, it is cleared up by the language of Mr. Pinckney's proposition of the 20th of August, which is more complete in its character, and in which he uses the words, "shall not be suspended *by the Legislature.*" It may be then safely affirmed, that at that time, and up to the 28th of August, when Mr. Pinckney again urged the propriety of securing the benefit of the Habeas Corpus in the most ample manner, the only department in which it was contemplated to vest the power of suspension was the Legislative. This conclusion cannot be resisted, when it is remembered that the only proposition introduced up to that time expressly provided for the suspension by the Legislature only. It was upon that day that the clause substantially as it now stands was moved by Mr. Morris.

The clause, as moved by Mr. Morris, was this: "The Privi-"lege of the Writ of Habeas Corpus shall not be suspended, "unless when, in cases of rebellion or invasion, the public safety "may require it." Mr. Pinckney's original proposition will be found *ante*, page 12.

The only substantial change made in the provision was to add the still further restriction, (when) "the public safety may "require it" after the word "invasion." It will be seen that Mr. Morris adopted the original proposition of Mr. Pinckney, making the above addition, which is immaterial as to the subject-matter now under discussion, and that he contemplated the application of the clause to the same department of the Government as was embraced by Mr. Pinckney's original proposition. If not, why did he adopt the same language, without making some such change as would have excluded such a conclusion?

"But," says Mr. Binney, "no such conclusion is to be "drawn, because the word 'Legislature,' used by Mr. Pinckney "in the beginning of his first proposition, was stricken out by "Mr. Morris." It is a mistake to say it was stricken out, for it was in Mr. Pinckney's original proposition only by relation to the first part thereof, and the clause is now found in the Constitution under that head which treats of the Legislative depart-ment of the Government, and immediately succeeding the restriction upon the power of Congress to prohibit the migration or importation of certain persons therein referred to, just as Mr. Pinckney's original clause connected it with the precedent restriction upon the Legislature as to the freedom of conscience and of the press, and is immediately followed by the restriction upon the power of Congress to enact bills of attainder or *ex post facto laws*. (See clause, *ante*, p. 6.) The original proposition of Mr. Pinckney followed, and was in the same clause with the prohibition upon the Legislature to pass laws on the subject of religion, or abridging the liberty of the press. The position of the present clause is in Article I, which treats of legislative powers and legislative restrictions, and is both preceded and followed by such restrictions. It bears the same relation to the word "Congress," in the first clause of Section 9, Article I, which Mr. Pinckney's clause bore to the word "Legislature" in his first proposition. With what show of plausibility can it be argued that Mr. Morris intended to abandon Mr. Pinckney's original proposition?

But Mr. Binney further contends that as Mr. Morris made the motion, and it was adopted by the Convention as an amendment to the fourth section of the XIth Article of the Constitution as it had been reported by the Committee of Five on the 6th of August, which was the Judiciary Article, therefore the inference is expressly negatived that it was the Legislative department to which the clause was to apply. The reasons which induced Mr. Morris to attach the clause to the Judiciary Article, cannot now be certainly stated. Yet as that clause provided for the trial of crimes in the states where they were committed, and that such trial should be by jury, it is probable he at first proposed to attach it to that section as being cognate, and in a legal point of view connected with it. The fourth section of the XIth Article referred to is substantially the same as the third clause of the second section of the Constitution as finally adopted.

A further examination of the history of the clause will show that the inference referred to is not only not expressly negatived, but, on the contrary, is strongly supported by it. The Convention having discussed and adopted the articles and sections separately and in detail, on the 8th of September, 1787, " it was " moved and seconded to appoint a committee of five to revise

" the style of, and arrange, the articles agreed to by the House,
" which passed in the affirmative.

" And a committee was appointed by ballot, of the Hon. Mr.
" Johnston, Mr. Hamilton, Mr. G. Morris, Mr. Madison, and
" Mr. King." (Elliott's Deb., Vol. I, p. 295.)

On the 12th of September the committee reported the Constitution as revised and arranged, placing the clause in question in its present position, and of course taking it out of the Judiciary Article. So it was adopted.

It is clear from this that the Committee on Style and Arrangement, in recasting the Constitution, did not deem the Judiciary Article the proper place for the clause. It is equally clear that they did not regard it as applicable to the Executive department, otherwise, when finding it in the wrong place, and intending to put it in the right one, as it was their duty to do, they would have arranged it under Article II., which treats of the Executive department. It is hardly to be supposed that if Mr. Morris had intended to modify Mr. Pinckney's original proposition so as to make it applicable to the Executive department, instead of the Legislative, he would have moved it as an amendment to the Judiciary Article. And it is equally difficult of belief that with this idea prominent in his mind, as it must have been if he made the changes supposed by Mr. Binney, he would have consented to its final arrangement under the Article relating to the Legislative department, pressed back, as it would be, by relation and by all fair rules of construction into the very position from which he had wrested it by taking it out of the hands of Mr. Pinckney.

But the action of the Committee on Style and Arrangement negatives any such inference. It was their duty to rearrange and recast the whole, in order to make its every part harmonize. They had to exercise their judgment and discrimination as to the proper place for each article. In doing so, they put this clause under the Legislative head.

The argument is rendered still more conclusive by the fact that Mr. Morris was himself one of the Committee of Five on Style and Arrangement, and in fact placed the clause where it is now found. He was not only one of the Committee of Five, but he actually wrote the Constitution as reported by that committee and adopted. He says, in a letter to Timothy Pickering,

of December 22d, 1814, speaking of the Constitution, " That in-
" strument was written by the fingers which write this letter."
Mr. Madison says, " The *finish* given to the style and arrange-
" ment of the Constitution fairly belongs to Mr. Morris."
(Letter to Mr. Sparks, April 8th, 1831.)

With these facts before us, it can be affirmed with the utmost
confidence, that Mr. Morris did not intend to abandon Mr.
Pinckney's proposition as to the department upon which the
restriction was imposed, but on the contrary, that he placed it
in such a position, and under such circumstances, as to remove
every possible doubt that his purpose was to apply it to the
Legislature.

Upon examining the history of the clause and the Constitution as it now stands, the reader will be prepared to judge of
the force of the extraordinary remark to be found on page 32
of the pamphlet, that " the present position of the clause in the
" Constitution is not of the least importance."

One of the rules laid down by Blackstone for interpreting the
will of the Legislature in a case of doubt is to examine the context. The history of legislation may also be brought forward
in order to clear up any ambiguity in respect thereto. If there
could be any doubt as to the true construction of the clause in
question, its position with reference to other parts of the Constitution is necessarily a subject of consideration. The manner in
which it was placed in its present location is also entitled to very
great weight. That excludes the possibility of its having fallen
there by accident. It is wedged in between two clauses which
hold it fast and control it. It is inseparably connected with the
first, and it is the link which binds the third to the first. (See
the three clauses, *ante*, p. 6.)

It will be perceived that as the clause immediately preceding
the one in question is a direct prohibition upon Congress, and is
the first restrictive clause, and as the clause succeeding it is
confessedly also a restriction upon Congress, but without again
introducing the word Congress, it necessarily relates back to the
first clause of the section and through the Habeas Corpus clause,
and thus brings down the word Congress through the Habeas
Corpus clause, and as an inseparable part of it. Otherwise it
would have been requisite to reintroduce the word Congress

for the proper construction of the sentence; that is, the word having been used in the first clause, and dropped in the second, it would necessarily have been reproduced in the third. The failure so to reproduce it proves that it was not dropped in the second, but was implied in reference to that as well as the third.

It is probably the first time in our history that an able and profound lawyer has gravely advanced the proposition, that the present position of any clause in the Constitution "is not of the "least importance."

However the fact may be as to any other, certainly such an assertion as to the Habeas Corpus clause by one whose reputation for learning and acumen in his profession was at all questionable, would argue a degree of boldness bordering very closely upon temerity.

It involves the reflection upon the framers of that instrument of their having been so reckless as to the effect of their work, and so faithless to the trust confided to them, that they pitched this most important safeguard to the liberties of the people hap-hazard into the Constitution without caring where it chanced to fall.

Fortunately the history of the manner in which it reached its present position, repels any such imputation. It shows that they had an intelligent understanding of what they were doing, and that they executed their purpose in the way most conducive to the protection and preservation of the liberties of the people.

That purpose was to place the restriction upon the exercise of the power of suspension upon the Legislative department, to which only the power was confided, and it was so effected as to exclude all possibility of implication that any such authority was intended to be conferred upon any other branch of the Government. Looking, then, to the history and position of the clause, it is clear that the restriction is applicable to Congress, and that necessarily involves the premise that they alone are invested with the power of suspension.

VIEWED IN THE LIGHT OF AUTHORITY.

Another light in which the pamphlet views this question is that of authority,—the language is this:

" The question of the power of Congress over this matter has " never been decided authoritatively, and it has never been " argued with any care, or perhaps argued at all, by a court or " by counsel in court. So far as authority goes it is a question " of first impression. There probably has been and still is " strong professional bias in favor of the power of Congress, " perhaps a *judicial bias*, if that be possible. It was not easy " to avoid the bias under the influence of English analogy, which " some preceding remarks were intended to disqualify; but " there is nothing on the point that is judicially authoritative." (Pamphlet, p. 36.)

It then proceeds, in the most summary manner, to brush away the opinion of Chief Justice Taney in the Merriman case.

Leaving the opinion of the Chief Justice to stand upon its own merits, it is proposed to inquire how far it is true that " there is nothing on the point that is judicially authoritative."

In Ex parte Bollman and Swartwout, 4 Cranch, 101, Chief Justice Marshall holds this language, " If at any time the public " safety should require the suspension of the powers vested by " this act in the courts of the United States, it is for the Legis- " lature to say so.

" That question depends on political considerations on which " the Legislature is to decide. Until the legislative will be " expressed, this Court can only see its duty, and must obey " the laws."

This is certainly the very highest judicial authority. But, it is said, that this was " altogether *obiter*," and is no authority.

It is worthy of consideration whether even an "*obiter*" of Chief Justice Marshall upon such a question would not be good authority. He spoke neither lightly nor loosely. A review of the case will show that he could not have spoken without reflection.

In the latter part of 1806, Burr's conspiracy reached its culmination. Gen. Wilkinson, with a view of strangling it in its early stages, had arrested certain persons in New Orleans as emissaries of Burr and accomplices in his treason. Two of them, Bollman and Swartwout, were sent by him to Washington City under arrest. On the 22d of January, 1807, Mr. Jefferson, then President, sent a message to Congress detailing the facts. On the 23d of January a bill was passed by the Senate suspending the privilege of the Writ of Habeas Corpus for three months in cases of persons charged with treason, or other high crime or misdemeanor endangering the peace, safety, or neutrality of the United States, who had been or should be arrested or imprisoned by virtue of any warrant or authority of the President of the United States, or from any person acting under the direction or authority of the President.

On the 26th of January the bill was communicated by the Senate to the House.

A motion was made by Mr. Eppes to reject it,—the purport of this motion being that the bill was so infamous as not to be worthy of consideration. This was warmly and ably discussed, and, upon the vote being taken on the question, "Shall the bill be rejected?" the vote was—yeas, 113; nays, 19. (Benton's Debates, Vol. III, p. 515.)

A reference to these debates will show that the subject was thoroughly examined. It was discussed as to the power of Congress under the Habeas Corpus clause—the proper construction of that clause—the right of the President to cause persons to be arrested in one district and transported to another,—the subordination of the military to the civil power, and the propriety of endeavoring to protect those who had made the arrests from civil liability therefor, by an act of Congress legalizing what had been done.

In February, 1807, the motion was made in the Supreme Court of the United States, at Washington City, for the Habeas Corpus in the cases of Bollman and Swartwout. Upon this motion a most elaborate argument was had upon the power and jurisdiction of the Court to issue the writ. Upon the 13th of February the motion was granted, and the opinion of the Court was delivered by Chief Justice Marshall. It was in the closing part of his remarks, and as a conclusive answer to all the objections made to the issue of the writ, that the Chief Justice uttered the language cited, *ante*, p. 20.

It is quite evident, from what fell from Johnson, Justice, in his dissenting opinion upon the motion, that the character of the transaction, as it related to the action of the Executive, did not

escape the attention of counsel, and it is almost certain that it
·was strongly pressed upon the Court in their speeches.

He says, in referring to the case of Burford, "I did not then
"comment at large on the reasons which influenced my opinion,
"and the cause was this: the gentleman who argued that cause
"confined himself strictly to those considerations which ought
"alone to influence the decisions of this Court. No popular
"observations on the necessity of protecting the citizen from
"Executive oppression; no animated address, calculated to enlist
"the passions or prejudices of an audience in defence of his
"motion, imposed on me the necessity of vindicating my opinion."
(Ex parte Bollman & Swartwout, 4th Cranch, p. 106.)

These remarks could have reference only to the manner in
which counsel had pressed the illegal and unauthorized action
of the Executive department in the matter of the arrests. It
is proper to remark that his dissent was simply predicated upon
the want of power in the Court sitting as the Supreme Court to
issue writs of Habeas Corpus. He did not deny the power to
the judges when holding the Circuit Courts. The writ being
issued and return made to it, a thorough discussion was again
had upon the question whether the prisoners were lawfully detained or not. On the 21st of February they were discharged,
the Chief Justice again delivering the opinion of the Court.

The discussion in Congress, the passage by the Senate of a
bill, the object of which was to legalize the arrests and transportation of Bollman and Swartwout, and the elaborate argument
of counsel, the importance of the questions involved, and the
anxiety of the friends of the Executive to obtain legal justification for what had been done, forbid the supposition that so
important an aspect of the matter did not present itself as that
of the department in which the power of suspension was reposed.

Had the Court decided that the power of suspension under
the Constitution resided in the Executive, then, according to
Mr. Binney's argument, the question could easily have been
settled, and the President would have been relieved from the
necessity of resorting to such indirection as an Act of Congress
for legal justification.

For 1st. The President could have decided that Burr's conspiracy was insurrection. In fact, Mr. Bidwell, in his

speech, says he had done so. "The first inquiry would naturally "turn upon the existence of a rebellion. On that point he had "no doubt. . . . . . The public notoriety of the fact was, "perhaps, sufficient evidence for the Legislature to act upon, if "necessary; but they had also the official statement of the "President to that effect." (Benton's Debates, Vol. III, p. 510.)

2d. The President had only to decide that the public safety required the suspension, and he and his friends would have been fully protected.

To suppose that this point could have escaped Mr. Jefferson and his friends, if there had been a shadow of foundation for it, is to impute to them a degree of dulness not often met with in advocates of Executive power.

The fact is, that all parties then concurred in the opinion that the power resided in Congress alone; and it is quite evident, that the Constitution was most carefully examined as to the whole subject.

If the principle now contended for so earnestly had any semblance of authority, it could not have been overlooked, for it lay at the very threshold of the investigation.

The subject-matter had grown out of arrests by the military power, and transportation to a different district from that in which the arrests had been made. The President had adopted the acts of his officer.

Chief Justice Marshall examined the Constitution in reference to the cases before him. He found that the power of suspension was so clearly in Congress, that it needed no argument, and he simply stated it as a proposition too plain for doubt. The examination of the case by any unbiassed mind can arrive at no other conclusion. In this view of the matter, the opinion of Chief Justice Marshall is in the highest degree judicially authoritative.

In Johnston v. Duncan et al., 1 Martin's Louisiana R., pp. 157–167, the question as to the legality of the martial law established by General Jackson in New Orleans during the memorable winter of 1815, came up before the Judges of the Supreme Court of Louisiana.

Judge Martin in delivering his opinion said : "This leads me "to the examination of the power to suspend the Writ of Habeas "Corpus, and that which it is said to include, of proclaiming "martial law as noticed in the Constitution of the United "States. As in the whole article cited, no mention is made of "the power of any other branch of the Government but the "legislative, it cannot be said that any of the limitations which "it contains, extend to any of the other branches. *Iniquum* "*est perimi de facto, id de quo cogitatum non est.* If, therefore, "this suspending power exist in the Executive (under whose "authority it has been attempted to exercise it) it exists without "any limitation—then the President possesses without a limita- "tion a power which the Legislature cannot exercise without a "limitation. Thus he possesses a greater power *alone* than the "House of Representatives the Senate and himself jointly. "Again, the power of repealing a law and that of suspending "it (which is a partial repeal) are legislative powers. For "*eodem modo, quo quid construitur, eodem modo destruitur.* As "every legislative power that may be exercised under the Con- "stitution is exclusively vested in Congress, all others are re- "tained by the several States."

Judge Derbigny says : "The Constitution of the United States, "in which everything necessary to the general and individual "security has been foreseen, does not provide, that in times of "public danger, the Executive power shall reign to the exclu- "sion of all others. It does not trust into the hands of a dicta- "tor the reins of government. The framers of that Charter "were too well aware of the hazards to which they would have "exposed the fate of the Republic by such a provision: and had "they done it, the States would have rejected a Constitution "stained with a clause so threatening to their liberties. In the "meantime conscious of the necessity of removing all impedi- "ments to the exercise of the Executive power, in cases of re- "bellion or invasion, they have permitted Congress to suspend "the privilege of the Writ of Habeas Corpus in those circum- "stances, if the public safety should require it. Thus far and "no farther goes the Constitution."

The decision of the Court was in accordance with these views.

This is judicial authority, and certainly it cannot be said that *the question* was not before the Court. Did Mr. Binney overlook this case, or does he not regard the decisions of the Supreme Court of Louisiana of that day as worthy of notice in the consideration of what is judicial authority?

But with the exception of a very brief and slighting allusion to Judge Story's remarks in his Commentaries on the Constitution, the pamphlet omits entirely allusion to two classes of authorities, which are certainly entitled to weight in the consideration of every question of constitutional jurisprudence. They are the opinions of text-writers, and the expressions of statesmen in the public councils, contemporaneously with the adoption of the Constitution, and since that time.

First, as to the authority of the text-books. Judge Story, in his Commentaries, says : " Hitherto, no suspension of the " Writ has been authorized by Congress since the establishment " of the Constitution. It would seem, as the power is given to " Congress to suspend the Writ of Habeas Corpus in case of " rebellion or invasion, that the right to judge whether the " exigency had risen, must exclusively belong to that body." (Story's Com., Sec. 1336.)

" The privilege of the Writ of Habeas Corpus shall not be " suspended (viz.: by Congress), unless when, in cases of " rebellion or invasion, the public safety may require it." (Note 15, Tucker's Blackstone, Vol. II, p. 134.)

A very excellent work was published by Mr. Hurd, in 1858, entitled, " A Treatise on the Right of Personal Liberty, and on the Writ of Habeas Corpus." It has the merit of being the only complete text-book on the subject. He says, " Rebellion " and invasion are eminently matters of national concern ; and " charged as Congress is, with the duty of preserving the " United States from both these evils, it is fit that it should " possess the power to make effectual such measures as it may " deem expedient to adopt for their suppression.

" In the discharge of this duty, it may provide for the arrest " and imprisonment of offenders or of suspected persons, and " forbid their release, while the exigency lasts, by either " State or Federal Courts. . . . . . This power has never been "exercised by Congress." (Hurd on Habeas Corpus, pages 133, 134.)

"This clause provides for the suspension of the Writ of "Habeas Corpus only in cases of rebellion or invasion, when "the public safety requires it; but Congress has never sus- "pended the Writ since the Constitution went into operation." (The Constitutional Text-book, by Furman Sheppard, published in 1856, p. 143.)

These are the opinions of eminent lawyers, and one of them a most distinguished Judge, given at a time when they were certainly free from any political bias. They are valuable, not merely for that reason, but also because they are the concurrence of the minds of impartial commentators, looking at the question with no other motive than to search for truth, and they evidence the fact that no other view had ever been taken prior to the present day.

But there is a current of authority found in the opinions expressed by the statesmen of the day when the Constitution was adopted, and running down through the history of the Government to within a very recent period, which is, perhaps, more potential than any other.

In the Massachusetts Convention, called to determine whether the Constitution should be ratified or not, the Habeas Corpus clause being under consideration on the 26th of January, 1788, "Dr. Taylor asked why this darling privilege was not "expressed in the same manner as in the Constitution of Massa- "chusetts? . . . He remarked on the difference of expression, "and asked why the time was not limited?

"Judge Dana said: The answer in part to the honorable gen- "tleman must be that the same men did not make both Consti- "tutions; that he did not see the necessity or great benefit of "limiting the *time*, supposing it had been as in our Constitution, "'not exceeding twelve months;' yet, as our Legislature can, "so might *Congress* continue the suspension of the Writ from "year to year. The safest and best restriction, therefore, "arises from the nature of the cases in which *Congress* are "authorized to exercise that power at all, namely, in those of "rebellion or invasion. These are clear and certain terms, facts "of public notoriety; and whenever these shall cease to exist,

" the suspension of the Writ must necessarily cease also. He
" thought the citizen had a better security for his privilege of
" the Writ of Habeas Corpus under the Federal than under
" the State Constitution; for our Legislature may suspend the
" Writ as often as they judge 'the most urgent and pressing
" occasions' call for it.

" Judge Sumner said, that this was a *restriction on Congress*
" that the Writ of Habeas Corpus should not be suspended,
" except in cases of rebellion or invasion. The learned Judge
" then explained the nature of the Writ. . . . . The privilege,
" he said, is essential to freedom, and, therefore, the power to
" suspend it is restricted. On the other hand, the State, he
" said, might be involved in danger; the worst enemy may lay
" plans to destroy us, and so artfully as to prevent any evidence
" against him, and might ruin the country, without the power
" to suspend the Writ was thus given. ' Congress have only
" ' power to suspend the privilege to persons committed by
" ' their authority. A person committed under the authority of
" ' the States will still have a right to the Writ.' " (2d Elliott's
Debates, 108.)

In the act of ratification by the Convention of New York is
this remarkable clause, among others, explanatory of their understanding of the Constitution: " That every person restrained of
" his liberty is entitled to an inquiry into the lawfulness of such
" restraint, and to a removal thereof, if unlawful; and that such
" inquiry and removal ought not to be denied or delayed, except
" when, on account of public danger, *the Congress* shall suspend
" the privilege of the Writ of Habeas Corpus.*

" Under these impressions, and declaring that the rights afore-
" said cannot be abridged or violated, and *that the explanations*
" *aforesaid are consistent with the said Constitution,* . . . .
" we, the said delegates, in the name and on behalf of the people
" of the State of New York, do by these presents assent to and
" ratify the said Constitution." (Supplement to Journal of the

---

* No proof can be more conclusive than this is as to the understanding
and intention of the framers of the Constitution. This action of the Convention is in itself a complete answer to the elaborate argument under consideration. No ingenuity can mystify it. No controversial skill can weaken or
destroy its force.

Federal Convention, published in Boston in 1819, pp. 428 and 431.)

The Convention of Rhode Island also ratified the Constitution with certain explanatory declarations; among them is the following:

"VII. That all power of suspending laws, or the execution "of laws, by any authority, without the consent of the repre- "sentatives of the people in the Legislature, is injurious to their "rights, and ought not to be exercised." (Idem, p. 455.)

In the debate in the Virginia Convention, Mr. Patrick Henry, in speaking of the 9th section, used this language:

"The design of the negative expressions in this section is to "prescribe limits beyond which the powers of *Congress* shall "not go. . . . . . . The first prohibition is, that the "privilege of the Writ of Habeas Corpus shall not be suspended, "but when, in case of rebellion or invasion, the public safety "may require it. It results clearly that, if it had not said so, "*they* could suspend it in all cases whatsoever." . . . . . (Elliot's Deb., Vol. III, p. 461.) See also remarks of Gov. Randolph, quoted *ante*, p. 9.

These were the declarations in four Conventions called for the ratification of the Constitution; and in that of New York, it will be observed, that it is expressly set forth, in their act of ratification, that the power of suspension is in Congress.

Mr. Hamilton was a member of the Federal Convention, and also of the New York Convention. It will scarcely be alleged that his jealousy of the Executive would have led him so far astray as thus to have sanctioned the declaration of the existence of power in Congress, which he, as a delegate to the Federal Convention, and a member of the Committee on Style and Arrangement, had vested in the President. Can it be said at this late day to citizens of New York that the power is in the President, when their act of ratification declares it to be in Congress, and they accepted, adopted, and have acted upon the Constitution with that construction, and without a voice anywhere dissenting from that interpretation, either then or for seventy years afterwards?

But passing down in the history of the Government we find the same views entertained, acted upon, and expressed by public men under circumstances which entitle them to very great weight.

The subject of the suspension of the Habeas Corpus was first discussed in Congress in 1807, when a bill for that purpose was introduced and passed by the Senate, but rejected by the House. This has already been referred to ; but the opinions then expressed as to the department in which the power was reposed, have a direct bearing upon the question of authority.

Mr. Jefferson was President, and the history of the transaction furnishes conclusive evidence that he did not, for a moment, claim the power as existing in his department, but conceded it to belong to the legislative.

Timothy Pickering, John Quincy Adams, and William B. Giles, were members of the Senate. Their names are mentioned as distinguished statesmen of their day. The Senate passed the bill entitled, " An Act to Suspend the Privilege of the Writ of " Habeas Corpus for a Limited Time in Certain Cases." It appears to have been a unanimous vote. The bill was reported by a committee composed of Messrs. Giles, Adams, and Smith of Maryland. (3d vol. Benton's Deb., 490.)

It is to be inferred that the President and the Senators from all the States concurred in this construction. The bill was sent from the Senate to the House of Representatives, and, although rejected by them, it was not for a moment doubted that the power of suspension, upon the occasions contemplated by the Constitution, appertained exclusively to the Legislative department. This is sustained by the following quotations from the speeches delivered in the House :

Mr. Burwell said, " If that be the case, upon what ground " shall we suspend the Writ of Habeas Corpus ? . . . . . " Nothing but the most imperious necessity would excuse us in " confiding to the Executive, or any person under him, the power " of seizing and confining a citizen, upon bare suspicion, for " three months, without responsibility for the abuse of such " unlimited discretion." . . . .

Mr. Elliott said, " We can suspend the Writ of Habeas Corpus " only in a case of extreme emergency. . . . . " But we shall be told that the Constitution has contemplated " cases of this kind, and, in reference to them, invested us with

" unlimited discretion. When any gentleman shall advance such
" a position, we shall meet him upon that ground, and put the
" point at issue." . . . .

Mr. Eppes said, "By this bill we are called on to exercise one
" of the most important powers vested in Congress by the Con-
" stitution of the United States. . . . . . . The words
" of the Constitution are, ' The privilege of the Writ of Habeas
" Corpus shall not be suspended, unless when, in cases of rebel-
" lion or invasion, the public safety may require it.' The word-
" ing of this clause of the Constitution deserves peculiar atten-
" tion. It is not in every case of invasion, nor in every case of
" rebellion, that the exercise of this power by Congress can be
" justified under the words of the Constitution. . . . . .
" The Constitution, however, having vested this power in Con-
" gress, and a branch of the Legislature having thought its
" exercise necessary, it remains for us to inquire, whether the
" present situation of our country authorizes, on our part, a
" resort to this extraordinary measure." . . . .

Mr. Varnum said, "I consider the country, in a degree, in
" a state of insecurity; and if so, the power is vested in Con-
" gress, under the Constitution, to suspend the Writ of Habeas
" Corpus." . . . .

Mr. Sloan said, "Had this measure been brought forward a
" month or six weeks ago, I should have voted for it." . . . .

Mr. Bidwell said, "Before the passing of any bill of this
" nature, the House ought to have satisfactory proof that a
" rebellion in fact existed (for there was no pretence of an inva-
" sion), and that the public safety required a suspension of the
" privilege of Habeas Corpus. By the terms of the Constitu-
" tion, both of these prerequisites must concur to authorize the
" measure." . . . .

Mr. J. Randolph said, "It appears to my mind like an oblique
" attempt to cover a certain departure from the established law
" of the land, and a certain violation of the Constitution of the
" United States, which, we are told, have been committed in this
" country. Sir, recollect that Congress met on the first of
" December, that the President had information of the incipient
" stage of this conspiracy about the last of September, that the
" proclamation issued before Congress met, and yet that no sug-

" gestion, either from the Executive or from either branch of
" the Legislature, has transpired touching the propriety of sus-
" pending the Writ of Habeas Corpus, until this violation has
" taken place. I will never agree in this sideway, to cover up
" such a violation, by a proceeding highly dangerous to the
" liberty of the country, or to agree that this invaluable privi-
" lege shall be suspended, because it has been already violated,
" and suspended too, after the cause, if any there was, for it has
" ceased to exist." . . . .

Mr. Smilie said, " A suspension of the privilege of the Writ
" of Habeas Corpus is, in all respects, equivalent to repealing
" that essential part of the Constitution which secures that prin-
" ciple which has been called the palladium of ' personal liberty.'
" If we recur to England, we shall find that the Writ of Habeas
" Corpus in that country has been frequently suspended. But
" under what circumstances ? . . . . We have
" taken from the statute of this country (England) this most
" valuable part of our Constitution. The Convention who framed
" that instrument, believing that there might be cases when it
" would be necessary to vest a discretionary power in the Exe-
" cutive, have constituted the Legislature the judges of this
" necessity ; and the only question to be determined now is,
" does this necessity exist ?" (3d vol. Benton's Deb., 504–514.)

On the 17th of February, 1807, the House of Representatives
proceeded to consider the motion of Mr. Broom, to wit : " Re-
" solved, that it is expedient to make further provision by law
" for securing the privilege of the Writ of Habeas Corpus to
" persons in custody, under or by color of the authority of the
" United States."

Mr. Broom said, " This privilege of the Writ of Habeas
" Corpus has been deemed so important that by the ninth sec-
" tion of the first Article of the Constitution it is declared that
" it ' shall not be suspended, unless when, in cases of rebellion
" ' or invasion, the public safety may require it.' Such is the
" value of this privilege that even the highest legislative body
" of the Union—the legitimate representatives of the nation—
" are not intrusted with the guardianship of it, or suffered to
" lay their hands upon it, unless when, in cases of extreme
" danger, the public safety shall make it necessary. . . . . .

" This constitutional provision was intended only as a check
" upon the power of Congress in abridging the privilege, but
" was never intended to prevent them from intrenching it around
" with sound and wholesome laws; on the contrary, it was ex-
" pected that Congress were prohibited from impairing at their
" pleasure this privilege,—that they would regard it as of high
" importance, and, by coercive laws, insure its operation." . .

Mr. Bidwell said, "The Constitution, by restricting the Legis-
" lature from suspending it, except when, in cases of rebellion
" or invasion, the public safety may require a suspension, had
" recognized it as a writ of right, and our statutes had autho-
" rized certain courts and magistrates to grant it."

Mr. G. W. Campbell said, " *This provision evidently relates*
" *to Congress*, and was intended to prevent that body from sus-
" pending by law the Writ of Habeas Corpus, except in the
" cases stated, and has no relation whatever to the act of an
" individual in refusing to obey the Writ,—such refusal or dis-
" obedience would not certainly suspend the privilege of that
" Writ, and must be considered in the same point of view as the
" violation of any other public law made to protect the liberty
" of the citizen." . . . .

Mr. Holland said, "But, sir, so far as respects the Habeas
" Corpus, *the suspension of it applies to the Legislature*, and not
" to persons.   The Constitution says, it shall not be suspended
" but in case of rebellion, or when the public safety requires it.
" *This prohibition manifestly applies to the Legislature*, and not
" to persons in their individual capacity." . . . . .

Mr. J. Randolph said, "The Writ of Habeas Corpus is the
" only Writ sanctioned by the Constitution. *It is guarded from*
" *every approach, except by the two Houses of Congress.*" (3d
vol. Benton's Debates, pp. 520–540.)

In 1842, in the debate on the bill to indemnify Gen. Jackson
for the fine imposed on him by Judge Hall, at New Orleans,
Mr. Bayard said, " Congress may indeed suspend the privilege
" of the Writ of Habeas Corpus, but cannot declare martial law
" to be the law of the United States, or of any part of them.
" . . . . . . The Constitution says, Congress shall have
" power to declare war, to raise armies, to provide a navy, to
" provide arms and munitions of war, and to make rules for the

" government of the land and naval forces. On these limited " and specific powers it has been inferred that Congress may " declare martial law. To avoid this very conclusion there is " an express provision in the very next section, among the re- " strictions on the powers of Congress, declaring that the remedy " of the Writ of Habeas Corpus shall not be suspended, unless " in cases of rebellion or invasion. . . . . . All Congress " can do, even in cases of rebellion or invasion, is to suspend " the privilege of the Writ of Habeas Corpus; and that can be " done by Congress only—not by an officer of the Government— " without its authority." (Vol. XIV, Benton's Debates, page 627.)

On January 14, 1843, the same subject was discussed in the House of Representatives.

Mr. Hunt said (after quoting the ninth section of the first Article of the Constitution, which provides that the privilege of the Writ of Habeas Corpus shall not be suspended, unless when, in cases of rebellion or invasion, the public safety may require it), "Who was to be the judge of that necessity? Was it the " President of the United States, or any subordinate officer in " command? No; it was the Legislature of the country that " was the judge, and the only judge of that necessity. He " supported the position by citing the practice of Mr. Jefferson, " who, in 1807, as President of the United States, applied to " Congress for a temporary suspension of the Writ of Habeas " Corpus for three months; which, however, was refused by the " House of Representatives, where the bill was defeated, which " had passed the Senate for that purpose."

In the House of Representatives, in the debate on the bill to indemnify General Jackson, January 2, 1844, Mr. Barnard said, "The Constitution gave Congress authority to pass laws " for the regulation of the army and navy of the United States, " and under that, Congress have passed laws for the government " of the army and navy and the militia. That code was appli- " cable to the officers and soldiers, and to the militia, when in " service; but it was not applicable to any other human being. " Congress itself could not proclaim martial law. *It might sus-* "*pend the Habeas Corpus Act,* but it could not suspend the " Constitution. A proclamation of martial law by the Congress

" of the United States would, of itself, be a violation of the
" Constitution." (Vol. XIV, Benton's Debates, p. 657.)

In an opinion delivered by Mr. Attorney-General Cushing,
upon the subject of martial law, and the suspension of the
Habeas Corpus, in February, 1857, growing out of a proclamation of martial law by the Governor of Washington Territory,
in order to suspend the Habeas Corpus, this language is used:
" The opinion is expressed by commentators on the Constitution,
"that the right to suspend the Writ of Habeas Corpus, and
" also that of judging when the exigency has arisen, belongs
" exclusively to Congress. . . . . . . It may be assumed, as a
" general doctrine of constitutional jurisprudence in all the
" United States, that the power to suspend laws, whether those
" granting the Writ of Habeas Corpus, or any other, is vested
" exclusively in the Legislature of the particular State."
(Opinions of Attorneys-General, Vol. VIII, p. 365.)

It is a question well worthy of consideration, whether, after
so long and continuous a stream of authority has been flowing
in this one direction, it can be necessary to go into any other
argument to prove this power to be vested in the Legislative
department. If the framers of the Constitution so understood
and intended it, that is an end to the controversy. That they
did so understand and intend is abundantly sustained by the
history of the clause and the authorities herein cited.

It would be a most remarkable instance of inaccuracy, if they
had used language which misled themselves and all other persons who examined the subject for a period of seventy years.
Such weight of authority would, in reference to almost any
other subject, have closed the door to question or doubt forever.

Is the statement " that so far as authority goes it is a question
" of first impression," borne out by the facts? It is true that
this remark has reference only to judicial authority. But this,
with the absence of any allusion to the proceedings of the conventions and of Congress, or the text-writers hereinbefore cited,
except a very slighting reference to Judge Story's Commen-
aries, would lead the reader who had not examined the subject
o infer that there was no aid to be had from the records of the
past, whereas a flood of light is poured in by authorities quite
as persuasive and conclusive as any judicial opinions could be,

however well considered. It would certainly have been more satisfactory to have had some explanation of these authorities in connection with the statement referred to, and before it was made.

In view of the authorities it is now affirmed, that so far from its being a question of first impression, it is in truth most clearly settled, and should be set at rest for all time.

DOES THE CONSTITUTION, BY ITS OWN TERMS, VEST THE POWER IN THE PRESIDENT?

Having disposed of the question of authority, the pamphlet proceeds to show that the Constitution, by its own *terms*, vests the power in the President. The propositions advanced may be stated thus:

1. That what the Constitution has ordained on this subject is all the law required for bringing it into operation.

2. The Constitution itself authorizes its suspension under conditions, and, therefore, suspension in the cases supposed is an Executive act, and it never can become anything but an Executive act; hence, Congress could not authorize it.

3. That the conditions of rebellion and invasion, and the demands of the public safety in such a conjuncture, are within the proper functions of the Executive department; that the President may establish them, and the power of denying the privilege for a season belongs wholly to his office, with the effect which the Constitution allows.

1. As to whether that which the Constitution has ordained is all the law required for bringing it into operation.

Suspension, practically, must be worked out somewhat in this manner. A man is arrested, charged with a crime; he applies to a State or Federal Court for a Habeas Corpus; the Court to which the application is made, finding that there is no law suspending the Habeas Corpus, grant the Writ; all officers, civil and military, are bound to obey it. It is a matter of every-day practice to release minors from the army by this Writ. Upon the issue of the Writ, and the return showing that the applicant is confined without a lawful ground of detention, the

Court is bound to order his discharge, and the officer is bound to yield obedience. On the contrary, if an act of suspension had been passed by Congress, the Court would examine the petition, and if the case appeared to be one of those in which the act was intended to operate, the Judge would refuse to grant the Writ. If, however, there should be a doubt about it, or for any reason the Court should have granted the Writ, when the return to it was made, and it appeared by the return that the Writ was improvidently issued, as being in contravention of the law of Congress, the Court would merely so decide, and remand the prisoner.

By reason of the Act of Congress, the confinement and detention would become lawful as regarded such persons as were within the purview of the Act, and the Courts would be bound so to decide, and deny the Writ in the first instance; or if they had issued it, they would refuse to discharge upon being informed by the return that the prisoner was held under the provisions of the act of suspension. This rule would prevail for so long a period as the conditions contemplated by the act continued to exist.

That would be the regular, as well as the most appropriate method of working out the suspension in all such places as the Courts were holding their sessions, free from mob or revolutionary violence and influence. This would be "denying," "deferring," "delaying," hanging up for such season as was provided by the act of Congress, in accordance with the Constitution.

When the courts could not sit, or for any reason, the officers who had custody of such prisoners were persuaded that harm would befall the Government by reason of their obedience to the Writ, if issued by a court, the act of Congress might authorize them to detain the persons so arrested for such length of time as the public exigency demanded, or to refuse even to obey the court in the making of any order in violation of the law. This would be another mode of working out the suspension.

But in either mode there must be a law, an act of Congress, as a rule of action both for the courts and the officers who may have custody of the arrested persons. They cannot take the *ipse dixit* of any one. Officers cannot detain a prisoner without authority of law in any case. Certainly it will not be pretended that each marshal, or jailer, or military officer, who may have a prisoner in custody, has the right, under the Constitution, to determine whether there is rebellion and invasion, and whether or not the public safety requires the Habeas Corpus to be suspended by him in the particular case. The confusion resulting from such a system is too evident to allow of any such interpretation.

Again, if the constitutional clause is all the law required for bringing it into operation, is it not then a law which all men are alike bound to obey and fulfil,—the President, the judges, the marshals, the jailers, the military officers, and all others? In that aspect of the matter the question becomes a judicial one.

The judges, when applied to for a Habeas Corpus, would have to inquire: 1. Whether there was a rebellion or invasion. 2. If they decided that either existed, they would have to inquire whether the public safety required the suspension or not. No officer can refuse to obey a lawful writ of a court; and, until an act of Congress is passed taking away the power from the courts to issue and enforce obedience to their authorized writs, all men must obey. When the writ was issued, and the prisoner brought into court, it would be purely a judicial question whether the case fell within the contemplation of the clause or not. The officer who held the prisoner in custody could not decide the question for the court.

" Our Constitution, on the contrary, speaks to all subordinate " authorities created by it. . . . . . The Constitution is " itself the authority, and all that remains is to execute it in " the conditioned case." (Pamphlet, page 21.)

Who are the " subordinate authorities" thus spoken to? And what is the conditioned case? Are they not the judges, the President, the marshals, and all other officers, civil and military? Is not the conditioned case given by the Constitution? The argument proves too much. It makes suspension the active operative law in the conditioned case, and of course renders it a judicial question, whether the case has arisen or not, that will not be contended for by any one.

The foregoing remarks are intended to show that an act of

Congress is necessary to bring into operation the principle of suspension provided for by the Constitution.

2. Is suspension, under the Constitution, an Executive act, and can it become nothing else than an Executive act?

It has already been contended, with what success the reader must determine, that if the question was left under the constitutional clause without an act of Congress, the suspension would really be a judicial, not an Executive act; or, if not solely judicial, it would be an act of the marshals, jailers, and other officers who happened to have the custody of the arrested persons, conjointly with the courts. In point of fact it would not and could not become an act of the President. He has no direct or immediate custody or control over the persons arrested under the law in reference to treason. They are in the custody of the law. They are to be held under the law, tried under the law, and punished or discharged under the law. He, as commander-in-chief of the army and navy, has prisoners of war under his control. This is by the law of nations and of war. But not so with persons who are not such prisoners. A man arrested for treason, or treasonable practices, is no more under the control or in the custody of the President than such as are detained for counterfeiting or robbing the mails, or any other crime of like character. Therefore, when a Writ of Habeas Corpus is issued by a court to a marshal or jailer, commanding him to bring before the court a prisoner, and the marshal or jailer refuses so to do, it is not the President who refuses to obey the writ, and thereby suspends the privilege, either personally or acting through the subordinate officer.

The act of suspension consists in the refusal to obey. That is simply and exclusively the act of the officer, and he is liable personally for all the consequences. The President is in no sense responsible for it, and his order is no protection to the officer.

It is unreasonable to say that an act which is to be performed by an officer of the law, who is to look to the law, and not to the President, for his rule of action, and who in his sphere is as independent of the President as the President is of him in the discharge of his duties, is an act of the President, and cannot be anything else.

It is assumed that when Mr. Binney uses the word "Executive" he means "President," and treats the terms as convertible. If, however, a distinction is to be drawn between "President" and "Executive," meaning by the first to designate the individual chief magistrate, and by the latter all executive officers of the Government who derive their appointment from the President, and whose duty it is to aid in the execution of the laws as well as the President, then the argument which has already been advanced as to suspension by them under the rule proposed recurs in full force.

It is not doubted that Congress might (and it would be in the highest degree proper), in the suspension act, impose certain duties upon the President, and invest him with certain discretionary powers as to time, place, classes of persons, and other circumstances connected with the suspension; but it is not less clear that they could in like manner confer similar powers and impose similar duties upon other officers, both civil and military, for the purpose of carrying the act into effect. Indeed it would be absolutely necessary that they should clearly define the duties of such officers in the premises, in order to protect them from liability for damages in civil actions, to guard the persons arrested from arbitrary oppression, and efficiently promote the public safety.

3. But it is contended that the establishment or declaration of the existence of rebellion and invasion, and the demands of the public safety, are within the proper functions of the Executive department of our Government, and therefore that the power of suspension belongs to the office of President, with the effect which the Constitution allows.

The first part of this proposition demands careful examination. The Constitution does not, in express terms, confer upon the President, or confide to him, the duty of deciding or declaring when the conditions of rebellion or invasion exist. Nor does it either expressly, or by implication, deny the power or duty to Congress.

The language in that instrument which connects him or his duties directly with either is the provision, "that the President "shall be commander-in-chief of the army and navy of the United "States, and of the militia of the several States when *called* into

" the actual service of the United States." That is when, by an act of Congress, they are *called* into actual service, he is commander. He cannot call into existence a corporal's guard without the authority of law.

Congress are alone authorized " to declare war," " to raise and support armies," " to provide and maintain a navy," " to make rules for the government and regulation of the land and naval forces," and " to provide for calling forth the militia to execute the laws of the Union, suppress insurrections, and repel invasions."

Under these provisions, it would seem to be fair to infer that Congress has the power either to decide for themselves or to vest the discretion of declaring when invasion or rebellion have occurred, in such officer as they might deem best for the public interest. This power was, in fact, exercised in the adoption of the act of 1792. The authority conferred by that act to call out the militia was to be executed by the President in the case of the obstruction to the laws, upon being notified of the occurrence by the Associate Justice or a District Judge of the proper court. This was the first act on the subject, and although passed, as Mr. Binney says, in " a spasm of jealousy," it was signed and acted upon by General Washington. It was repealed in 1795, and a substitute passed, by which the President was authorized to call out the militia when the laws of the United States were opposed, or their execution obstructed by combinations too powerful to be suppressed by the ordinary course of judicial proceedings, or by the powers vested in the marshals.

Mr. Binney considers the act of 1795 as very potent proof of the power and duty of the President in this matter, but points out no reason why the act of 1792 was not quite as conclusive as to the power of Congress to vest the discretion in any other officer, and especially in a United States Judge.

The case of Martin *v.* Mott, 12 Wheaton, 19, certainly does not see in the act of 1795 anything more than an authority to the President to call out the militia when the exigency had arisen, and it only decides that which is a well-recognized rule of law, that when a statute provides that an act shall be done by any person upon his own judgment as to the contingency having arisen, no one can go behind his decision. Mr. Justice

Story, in delivering the opinion of the Court, said: " The power " thus confided to the President is, doubtless, of a very high " and delicate nature. . . . . . If it be a limited power, the " question arises, by whom is the exigency to be judged of and " decided ? . . . . . We are all of opinion that the authority to " decide whether the exigency has arisen, belongs exclusively to " the President, and that his decision is conclusive upon all " other persons. . . . . . The law does not provide for any " appeal from the judgment of the President. . . . . . When- " ever a *statute* gives a discretionary power to any person, to be " exercised by him upon his own opinion of certain facts, it is a " sound rule of construction that the *statute* constitutes him the " sole and exclusive judge of the existence of these facts ; and " in the present case we are all of opinion that such is the true " construction of the act of 1795."

Will this be called an " *obiter ?* " It decides that the power of the President to declare the existence of invasion is derived from the *statute*, and as the *statute* had given him discretionary power, the exercise of that power was conclusive.

So far as the action of Congress is concerned, the " voice " of the act of 1792 was to the effect that Congress could vest the power of deciding as to the fact of rebellion in what officer they saw fit; and the case of Martin v. Mott decides, that as to invasion, the power of the President in this regard springs from the authorization of the act of 1795.

It being established that Congress may either decide for themselves, or vest the discretion of deciding when rebellion or invasion exists, in any officer they may deem best for the public interest, and there being no exclusive power in the President under the Constitution so to decide, by virtue of his office, the argument based upon the assertion of such power in him falls to the ground. To infer that, because the President was authorized by the *act of Congress* of 1795 to declare the existence of rebellion or invasion, he was also empowered to suspend the Habeas Corpus under the Constitution, is to admit that, because the act of 1792 vested the same discretion in a judge, like power of suspension in the same case was given to the judge. The statement of this proposition is its own refutation.

This matter of the President's peculiar, inherent, self-supporting constitutional authority to decide upon and declare the existence of rebellion or invasion, with the deduction from it, is therefore out of the case.

The fallacy as to Executive power under this clause has its origin in the erroneous assumption that the "clause" is enlarging instead of restrictive in its character, and that the President derives his power from *the Constitution* to decide or declare when rebellion or invasion exists. It is not intended to deny that the President may, when the conditions of rebellion or invasion have occurred, take such precautionary measures, based upon the facts as they exist, and subject to the future action of Congress, as may be demanded by the public safety. Nothing is either affirmed or denied in reference to the power of the President in such an emergency, as it does not belong to the present discussion.

The position now taken goes no farther than merely to assert that the power of declaring the existence of rebellion or invasion belongs, constitutionally, to Congress; that they can vest the discretion of deciding upon the same facts in any officer they may deem best; and that the power of the President to declare their existence authoritatively and conclusively, comes not from the Constitution, but from the act of Congress; and hence the error as to his power to suspend the Habeas Corpus, predicated upon the mistake as to his authority in regard to the declaration of the existence of rebellion or invasion, is readily and easily comprehended.

The proposition that the "clause" is a restriction instead of a grant of authority, has already been discussed, *ante*, p. 8–11.

If it is a restriction, not a grant of power, and the power to suspend is derived to Congress from other parts of the Constitution, and especially from the clause authorizing them to provide for the suppression of insurrection, and the repelling of invasion, it is clear that the Habeas Corpus clause is not a law, self-executive and becoming operative by way of suspension, when the contemplated conditions exist, but that it is a prohibition applicable to Congress only, and leaving it to their legislative discretion to decide whether the contingencies provided for have arisen or not, and making it their duty to exercise the remnant of power left in them, upon the occurrence of the required conditions.

The admission, however, that the clause is a grant of power, instead of a restriction, upon that granted elsewhere, does not materially affect the question of the exclusive right of Congress. For, if any ellipsis is to be supplied, so as to make the sense complete, the materials for the addition are to be drawn from the ordinary rules of construction governing in such cases: such as analogy, position, context, judicial and contemporaneous, official and historical construction. Apply these rules, and the words to be added are, "And then it may be suspended *by* "*Congress.*" So decided is the argument, from position and context, that no text-writers, or other persons, whether in the State Conventions, or Congress, or judges, or lawyers, prior to the year 1861, ever suggested a doubt about it.

It is immaterial, therefore, whether the clause is regarded as enlarging or restrictive. For, if the latter, it is a qualification of power granted by a preceding clause to Congress. If the former, taken in connection with the preceding and succeeding provisions, it is a grant of power to Congress, limited by certain specific conditions.

THE PARLIAMENTARY DOCTRINE.

A considerable portion of the pamphlet is addressed to what is called the Parliamentary doctrine. The effort is made to establish the proposition that the "clause" is a "departure from "the English Constitution and rule," and that they are thus set aside, "as a safe analogy in the application of the clause "finally adopted." This line of argument is adopted, because it is admitted, that if the analogy of the English Constitution is applied to ours, it will inevitably carry the power into the Legislative, to the exclusion of the Executive department.

To determine to what extent it was a departure, and how far it is requisite to look to the English system, in order to arrive at correct conclusions, it is proper to take a brief notice of the English principle, as it existed in the mother country, and was drawn from that source into, and adopted by the Colonies first, the States afterwards, and finally by the framers of our Constitution.

The English people always maintained and asserted, "that "no freeman ought to be committed or detained in prison, or "otherwise restrained by the command of the King, or Privy "Council, or any other, unless some cause of the commitment,

" detainer, or restraint be expressed, for which, by law, he ought
" to be committed, detained, or restrained."*

The Writ of Habeas Corpus furnished the remedy against the
violation of this right in England. This was a common law
writ. It sprang from no statute. The struggle of the people
with the Crown for the maintenance and vindication of the principle resulted in its full acknowledgement and establishment by
the Magna Charta during the reign of King John. But it was
necessary to secure the right from executive encroachment
through servile judges, by some stringent and severe enactments. This gave rise to several acts of Parliament, the more
important of which were the 16 Charles I., 31 Charles II., and,
at a later period, 56 George III. These acts only protected
the people in the enjoyment of the common law right, by the
enactment of severe penalties for its violation, or for the refusal
or denial of the Habeas Corpus. They conferred no right not
already existing, but merely guarded and protected more efficiently the remedy. The right itself, and the privilege or right
to the remedy (the Writ of Habeas Corpus), were both common
law rights.† The only qualification of either was also a common

* The general principle seems to have had its advocates long prior to
the English era. About eighteen centuries ago, when Porcius Festus and
King Agrippa were examining the Apostle Paul, who had appealed from the
provincial court to the Roman Emperor, the former said: "It seemeth to me
"unreasonable to send a prisoner, and not withal to signify the crimes laid
"against him." (Acts, Chapter XXV, verse 27.)

† "It is a very common mistake, and that not only among foreigners, but
many from whom some knowledge of our constitutional laws might be ex-
pected, to suppose that this statute of Charles II. enlarged in a great degree
our liberties, and forms a sort of epoch in their history ; but, though a very bene-
ficial enactment, and eminently remedial in many cases of illegal imprisonment, it introduced no new principle, nor conferred any right upon the subject.
From the earliest records of the English law, no freeman could be detained in
prison except upon a criminal charge or conviction, or for a civil debt. In the
former case it was always in his power to demand of the Court of King's Bench
a writ of *habeas corpus ad subjiciendum*, directed to the person detaining him
in custody, by which he was enjoined to bring up the body of the prisoner,
with the warrant of commitment, that the Court might judge of its sufficiency,
and remand the party, admit him to bail, or discharge him, according to the
nature of the charge.

"This writ issued of right, and could not be refused by the Court. It was
not to bestow an immunity from arbitrary imprisonment, which is abundantly
provided in Magna Charta (if indeed it were not much more ancient), that

law principle, to wit, that Parliament, and Parliament alone, could suspend the privilege of the Writ, if they chose so to do, by the enactment of a law for that purpose.

Thus stood the English law when the Colonies were founded, and, in the language of the Continental Congress of 1774, " Our " ancestors who first settled these Colonies were, at the time of " their emigration from the mother country, entitled to all the " rights, liberties, and immunities of free and natural born sub- " jects within the realm of England."

Lord Chatham, in his argument before the House of Lords against the doctrine of taxation without representation, in 1766, said, " The Colonies are equally entitled with yourselves to all " the natural rights of mankind, and the peculiar privileges of " Englishmen, equally bound by the laws, and equally partici- " pating of the Constitution of this free country. The Ameri- " cans are the sons, not the bastards of England." These doc- trines have been universally recognized throughout the United States as true.

The principles, as to the freedom of the people, were the same in the Colonies as in England; also the principle that the power of suspension of the privilege of the Habeas Corpus was exclusively vested in the Legislative department, and explicitly and pointedly denied to the Executive department, was the law of the Colonies as well as of the mother country.

When the Colonies threw off their allegiance to Great Britain the principles of the common law still prevailed, and the powers which had previously resided in the Parliament became vested

the statute of Charles II. was enacted, but to cut off the abuses by which the Government's lust of power and the servile subtlety of Crown lawyers had impaired so fundamental a privilege." (Hallam's Constitutional History, page 500, chapter 13.)

" The *Habeas Corpus* is a common law writ, and has been used in England from time immemorial just as it is now. The statute of 31 Car. 2, c. 2, made no alteration in the practice of the courts in granting these writs (3 Barn. & Ald. 420–2; Chitty Reps. 207). It merely provided that the judges in vaca- tion should have the power which the courts had previously exercised in term time (1 Chitty's Gen. Prac. 586), and inflicted penalties upon those who should defeat its operation. The common law upon this subject was brought to America by the colonists; and most, if not all the States, have since enacted laws resembling the English statute of Charles II. in every principal feature." (Passmore Williamson's case, 2 Casey (Penna. State Reports), p. 16.)

in the legislative bodies of the respective Colonies, and the restrictions upon the King fell upon the Executive departments respectively so far as they were applicable.

Thus the proposition is deduced that, from the time of the Declaration of Independence, and up to the adoption of the Constitution of the United States, the right of freemen to the Habeas Corpus existed in the respective States just as it did in England; that the Legislative department in each, and it alone had the power of suspension, having inherited this function with all others which had belonged to the British Parliament; and that the non-existence of power in the Executive department was a part of the organic or fundamental law as it was in England. Of course it is not intended to deny that these principles might have been modified by State Constitutions.

Such were the general principles when the framers of the Constitution met together. No one can doubt that they were legislating with reference to matters as they then stood. They knew what the common law of England was, as applied to King, Parliament, and people, and that it applied to the Executive departments, Legislative departments, and the people of the several States, in the same manner as in England, except so far as the change of circumstances had modified it. In this regard there was no modification. They incorporated this great principle of the common law of non-suspension into the Constitution with no change, except to enlarge upon it as drawn from England, in favor of liberty, by limiting the power of suspension to occasions "when, in cases of rebellion or invasion, the public "safety may require it."

In all other respects, whether as regards the right of freemen or the Writ, or the privilege of the Writ, or the rules and doctrines applicable to the subject, in its every phase, they were left as brought from the mother country, and planted in the Colonies and carried into the new relation of independent States. Nor is there a single word in the Constitution which modifies, or alters, or changes the common law principle, that the power of suspension appertains to the Legislative department.

Mr. Binney says of the clause, " It is un-English, because it " ties up the legislative power as well as all other power; and " it is American, because it is of American origin, and is a con- " servative of personal freedom in general, and also of the public

" safety, in times of imminent internal danger of a specific cha-
" racter." Is this true in point of fact? It is the incorpora-
tion of a principle drawn entirely from English constitutional
law, with a limitation or restriction added, which leaves the
English principle in every respect in full force whenever the
conditions exist which authorize the exercise of the power of
suspension.

In other words, the moment the case of rebellion or invasion
intervenes, and the public safety requires it, the restriction dis-
appears, and every principle of the British Constitution springs
into full life and vigor as applicable to this subject. A rebellion exists, and the power of suspension *ipso facto* is, in every
respect, the English power of suspension.

It is peculiarly English also in this, that while the Parliament
have the power of suspension, it has been usual to exercise it
only when it was deemed best for the public safety, during
foreign and domestic disturbances. Their practice corresponds
with our constitutional restriction.

The only substantial difference, then, between our Constitution
and the English is, that what Parliament may do at any time
the proper department of our Government may do only at certain specified times, and that the restriction is but the enactment of their practice as a part of our organic law. By
their law, asserted and reasserted, established by everything
that can render a fundamental principle inviolably sacred, and
so endeared and cherished as to put the head of any sovereign
in peril who would encroach upon the right of his meanest subject in this respect, the King of England is prohibited from the
unlawful detention of any man, however vile or obscure.

The King is the Executive of England. The framers of the
Constitution were fresh from the struggle of the War of Independence. They had based their justification upon his illegal
and despotic acts. It was Executive power which had oppressed
their forefathers, and which had roused themselves to the highest
pitch of desperation in resistance to its aggressions.

They saw the value of the principle of the Habeas Corpus in
the English system as a protection against Executive power,
and adopted it with one addition in favor of the liberty of the
people; namely, a restriction of the power of suspension upon
the Legislative department, in which alone it was vested. This

is the only departure from the English principle. Its extent, however, can be appreciated when the fact is adverted to that our constitution upon this subject is but the enactment of their constitution and practice combined.

Enough has been said to show how utterly impossible it is to discard English analogy in considering this subject, as also to test the soundness of the objections to this mode of construction. The analogy is neither defective nor deceptive. It is the only one we have, and is the source whence the principle and every-thing connected with it have been drawn. We can as readily discard our language, or ignore our English blood. With it, the subject is simple and easy of comprehension; without it, we are lost in a labyrinth of vague and bewildering speculation.

Mr. Binney presents the matter in another light which demands notice. On page 35, he says: "If the clause in the " Constitution had said of the WRIT of Habeas Corpus, or of a " Habeas Corpus Act, enacted, or to be enacted, what it says of " the PRIVILEGE of the Writ, there would have been some ground " for the argument that a Writ of Habeas Corpus and a Habeas " Corpus Act, *being the work of the Legislature*, the suspension " of the Writ or Act should be made by the Legislature also."

This is a statement that *the Writ of Habeas Corpus* and the Habeas Corpus Acts are both legislative in their origin. A moment's reflection will detect the error conveyed by this lan-guage. Habeas Corpus *Acts* are the work of Legislatures. But the *Writ* of Habeas Corpus, as it prevails in the several States, has *not* necessarily its foundation in any legislative act, but in the common law. The legislative acts in reference to it only secure its benefit or privilege against corrupt or tyrannical judges, and compel its issue and obedience to it under severe penalties. Hence, if the clause had only spoken of the " Writ of Habeas Corpus," the language would not have been sufficiently comprehensive, as it might possibly have been held not to apply to the provisions of legislative acts.

It would have fallen equally short of the mark, if it had spoken of a Habeas Corpus Act, enacted, or to be enacted, for then it might have been held not to apply to the common law right to the Writ of Habeas Corpus.

Either form would only have covered half the ground. The language used expresses most appropriately and accurately the restriction intended to be imposed, comprehending alike the benefit of the Writ under the common law and also under any legislative act.

The Writ of Habeas Corpus has its derivation from three different sources : 1. The common law, which prevails throughout the several States composing the Federal Union.* 2. The Habeas Corpus Acts of the several States. 3. The act of Congress, authorizing the issue of the Writ.

Both the common law principle and that of all Habeas Corpus Acts have the same and but one purpose, and that is, to confer upon arrested persons the *benefit* or *privilege* of the Writ. Whether that benefit or privilege flows from the common law, or a Habeas Corpus Act, it is the purpose to be affected—the right to be secured—the thing to be accomplished. "Privilege," as used, is the generic term, comprehending all forms of enjoyment of the Writ, from whatever source, or in whatever manner derived. It embraces the Writ alike, as derived from the common law, and from legislative acts, whether of Congress, or of the several States, and is to be taken as if it had spoken expressly of all of them. Hence, if there is ground for the argument upon the hypothesis put by Mr. Binney, it will be seen that it is not weakened by the language which was actually adopted, but rather, that as in one aspect the enjoyment of the privilege might flow from or be secured by a legislative enactment, it would require legislation to suspend it.

THE DOCTRINE OF NECESSITY.

The pamphlet under consideration does not rest the claim for the power of the President upon either martial law or the doctrine of necessity. But it is urged by many persons that unless this power is vested in the Executive, the Government might be destroyed before Congress could be assembled; that there are occasions when the safety of the nation demands its exercise by the President.

* It is not intended to state that there is a common law of the United States in their relation as a Federal Union. But reference is had to the common law which prevails in each State, as it was imported from England, except in so far as it has been modified by Federal or State Constitutions, or statutory law, or by the altered condition of the people.

Let it be admitted. Is that a reason why the Constitution should be made to mean what was not intended? It was conceived some months ago, that the safety of the nation required the increase of the army and navy. There was no act of Congress authorizing it. The President took the responsibility. Did any one imagine, because the preservation of the Government required it, therefore the President had the constitutional power? It was admitted on all hands he had not, and his justification was to be found in the subsequent ratification by Congress.

It will not be denied that there are occasions which seem to call for extreme measures; when the Executive department may be strongly pressed to go to the utmost verge of doubtful power. All that can be said when that power is transcended is, that what is then done should be viewed with reference to the surrounding circumstances, and if they demonstrate the necessity and propriety of the course of the President, his acts should receive kind and generous consideration at the hands of those whose rights and interests he intended to guard and protect.

But because an act was done of necessity before Congress could be called together, that does not prove that it should be continued after Congress has been for weeks or months in session; nor does it engraft any new principle on the Constitution.

If Congress refuse to do their duty, the fault lies with them, but the President cannot usurp their powers. If this argument of the safety of the State is to furnish the rule of action for the Executive department, then Congress becomes a useless and cumbrous piece of machinery, and the sooner it is dispensed with the better; but along with it must go the Constitution. That instrument was specially intended to obviate and exclude any such appeal. It is written law, and was intended to prevent the exercise of arbitrary power in such emergencies as would tempt those in office to encroach upon the liberties of the people. The Constitution knows no "higher law" than its own plain precepts. That doctrine was born later down in the life of the nation. It is an excrescence thrown out in the heat of sectional and fanatical strife. It is neither Scriptural nor constitutional. It sweeps away all landmarks, human and Divine, and would carry us back into chaos—moral, social, and political.

But there is no such necessity, and no such dilemma as that supposed. Congress can, by general law, provide for suppressing insurrection, and repelling invasion, when they occur. They did so in 1795, and again in the extra session of 1861. The suspension of the Habeas Corpus is clearly one of the means which may be used constitutionally for that purpose; and, if they see fit, they can authorize its suspension on such occasions when the public safety may require it.

Another form of putting this derivation of the claim from necessity, adopted by some persons, is, that during war, foreign or insurrectionary, martial law supersedes the civil law.* A recent writer, in the "North American Review," of October, 1861, defines martial law to be "that military rule and autho-"rity which exists in time of war, and is conferred by the laws of "war, in relation to persons and things under and within the scope "of active military operations in carrying on the war, and which "extinguishes or suspends civil rights and the remedies founded "upon them for the time being, so far as it may appear to be "necessary, in order to the full accomplishment of the purposes "of the war." Where that military rule is to be found, in what code, what are its limits, who is to declare it, and who to repeal it, are questions that have never yet been answered.

Jacobs's Law Dictionary furnishes this definition: "The law "of war—that depends upon the just but arbitrary power and "pleasure of the King or his lieutenant. He useth absolute "power, so that his word is law."

In ordinary times the man would be deemed irrational who affirmed that we are liable to have any such law imposed upon us. The power of the President to call out the forces required to suppress insurrection, or repel invasion, comes from the act of Congress. The organization of the army and navy, the time and manner of their enlistment, the rules and articles of war for their government, down to the most minute particular,

---

* A very able pamphlet on the subject of martial law was published by the Hon. S. S. Nicholas, of Kentucky, in the year 1842. It has been republished within the past year with some additions, and should be read by every one who may wish to arrive at a just conclusion upon this subject.

His devotion to the preservation of the Union and the Constitution, and his eminence as a jurist, alike entitle his voice to be heard and his opinions to be esteemed by his countrymen.

are provided and enacted by Congress. It is under the authority of laws of Congress that every act is done in the course of a war. Is the power of the creature paramount that which created him? A stream cannot rise higher than its source. The Constitution says, Congress may suspend the Habeas Corpus. They create an army to suppress insurrection, but do not choose to suspend the Habeas Corpus. Can any general, whether commander-in-chief, or a subordinate, take upon himself to do that which those who brought him into existence did not authorize? Yet this is suspending the Habeas Corpus by martial law. The King of Great Britain cannot proclaim or establish martial law in his dominions.* Has the President more unlimited arbitrary power than the King of Great Britain? If the President can proclaim or establish martial law, what becomes of Articles III., IV., V., and VI., of amendments to the Constitution? Read them carefully, *ante*, page 6. They must first be abrogated before this new dogma can be inaugurated.† They were provided for the express purpose of fencing in and restraining any such dangerous and injurious tendencies. No articles could, perhaps, have been better or more explicitly framed for the protection of the liberty of the people; and it requires but a calm and impartial perusal of the whole Constitution to. see that this doctrine of the right of the Executive department to establish martial law has not the shadow of foundation there, but, on the contrary, is repugnant alike to its spirit and letter.

* Some remarks of Mr. Hargrave, in reference to the power of the King of Great Britain to proclaim martial law, will be found printed in the Appendix. They are commended to the careful attention of the reader.

† Many persons, and some of them by no means unlearned in the law, have recently advanced the proposition that there are occasions when it is justifiable to violate one part of the Constitution in order to preserve another. There is an authority to sustain that view to even a greater extent, perhaps, than they contend for. It is probably due to candor that such an authority should not be omitted in a discussion upon the suspension of the Habeas Corpus. On an occasion of the discussion of the suspension of the Habeas Corpus in the Irish Parliament, that distinguished constitutional jurist, Sir Boyle Roche, said, "It would surely be better, Mr. Speaker, to give up, not only a *part*, but, if necessary, even the *whole* of our Constitution, to preserve *the remainder!*" (Sketches by Sir Jonah Barrington, Judge of the High Court of Admiralty, Ireland, page 139.)

GENERAL REMARKS.

Recurring to the principles of construction, as applicable to the "Habeas Corpus" clause, it will be seen that the claim of the power of suspension for the Executive department is not sustained by either the plain rendering of the language or the spirit of the Constitution; that it is negatived by English analogy and the common law as it existed in the States at the time of its adoption; that it is contravened by the history of the clause in the Convention, and contemporaneous explanations of the members of that and the State Conventions, and by the uniform current of authority to be derived from the expressions of jurists, text-writers, and statesmen, from the foundation of the Federal Union down to the year 1861.

It is none the less clear that the power of suspension is vested in Congress, and in no other department. They are to exercise it as any other power conferred by the Constitution; that is, by passing a law, providing how, when, where, by whom, and for what length of time the privilege of the Writ is to be suspended, and as to what persons it shall be applicable. It is their duty, when doing so, to provide such guards and checks as may be requisite for the protection of the people against arbitrary and capricious arrests and detention, and to restrain those who, clothed with authority, may be disposed to violence or oppression. Nothing can be fraught with greater danger to the liberties of the people than subjection to the exercise of unregulated power of seizure and incarceration by innumerable officers, civil and military, scattered over all parts of the country.

It is not to be desired that any authority should be taken from the President which is given to him by the Constitution. The experience of seventy years has demonstrated the wisdom of the framers in the establishment and organization of the Executive department. But it has also shown the necessity for confining each department to the exercise of its own peculiar and appropriate functions.

Every violation of law, whether moral or governmental, has its attendant evil. The act of to-day becomes a precedent for to-morrow. A deflection from the line of rectitude, however slight in the first instance, involves the danger of still greater departures in the future. That which might have been in the highest degree commendable, if authorized, may afterwards be relied upon as justifying the gravest and most unpardonable wrongs.

One department of Government transcends its constitutional powers in what it deems a case of extreme necessity. The act evokes suspicion, distrust, and jealousy on the part of the other departments. It loosens the constraining force of the Constitution on all branches of the Government. The danger is, that when one ligament is broken, others will become relaxed, and, after a time, they will, one by one, be cut asunder, until the Constitution ceases to exist, except in name.

But not alone is evil to be apprehended from the violations on the part of the departments of the Government being thus induced. The people have always been watchful and jealous of the exercise by their rulers of powers not clearly granted. Each unauthorized act weakens the confidence of the people in their form of Government. As confidence is withdrawn, respect and affection fade. Prejudice against an act of violation attaches itself more or less to the officer to whom it is attributed, and, by an inflexible law of human nature, to the authority under which he claims his power. When these vicious influences have prevailed for a sufficient length of time, the people will be ready to yield to the counsels of evil-minded leaders, who, instead of seeking to restore the Government to its pristine integrity, by lawful and peaceable means, bend all their energies to impel their followers into the vortex of revolution and civil war.

These are some of the evils to be apprehended from any violation of the Constitution; and there is no one feature of it about which the people are more sensitive than that which relates to personal liberty. It is of the utmost importance that even a doubtful power should not be exercised in a point so wounding to their sensibilities.

It is to be most earnestly and devoutly hoped that no future occasion will arise when any resort to the suspension of the Habeas Corpus will be deemed requisite by any one. But, if it should, then, it is trusted, that the members of Congress of the day will have the firmness and manliness to meet the question, and, if necessary, provide such a law as is required by the public safety and warranted by the Constitution.

APPENDIX.

———

"Hargrave's Jurisconsult Exercitations," Vol. I., page 399.
Opinion in Irish case involving Martial Law.

The following small article includes, in some degree, matter of very high importance, which, though of great notoriety in Ireland where the transaction occurred, is not so generally known among us in England. It relates to the case of Mr. Cornelius Grogan, an Irish gentleman of large fortune, in the County of Wexford, who, during the horrid rebellion in that part of Ireland, in 1798, was taken for high treason, under the circumstance of there having been a previous proclamation authorizing martial law, in aiding the rebels, and was tried by a Court of Officers, and, being found guilty, was put to death on the judgment of that Court; and was, shortly after his death, attainted of high treason, by act of the Irish Parliament.

"Upon the case thus generally stated, with a view to the trial of rebels by martial law, it is proper to add that, in 1799, an Irish act of Parliament was passed, which, *in effect*, appears to recognize that it is a part of the Royal *prerogative*, during the time of rebellion, to authorize the King's general and other commanding officers *to punish rebels according to martial law, by death or otherwise, as to them shall seem expedient.* That an act of Parliament may, for more effectually suppressing rebellion, so extend trial by *martial law*, and so also give to generals, and other commanding officers, a discretion of punishing rebels, found guilty upon such trial, either with *death, or indefinitely in any other way*, is not to be doubted; for, when such an act is passed, though judges or others should ever so strongly feel, either its incongruity with the principles of our law, or its harsh latitude otherwise, the act must operate, till it be revoked by the same high authority as engrafts it on the law of England. But the question which forced itself, in a great degree, on the author's mind, when he was called upon professionally to write his opinion, in answer to those who consulted him for the purpose of seeking a repeal of the Grogan attainder, was,—whether, independently of the express warrant of an act of Parliament, and on the mere ground of prerogative power, authority could be given against persons taken into custody for high treason during the heat of rebellion, to try them by martial law for their offence, and to punish them either by death, or in any other way, at the discretion of the court martial so trying them. Looking to that question, he could not forbear avowing how his mind was affected. But he so avowed himself, under a conviction that martial law to such an extent was not the law of England, without an express act of Parliament. He saw the right of putting rebels to death in battle while the battle lasted. He also saw the right to arrest those found in actual rebellion, or duly charged with being traitors, and to have them imprisoned for trial and punishment according to the law of treason. But he could not see that trying and punishing rebels according to martial law was, when Mr. Grogan was tried and put to death, part of the English law, as it was administerable in England, or even as it was administerable in Ireland. On the contrary, he saw such a prerogative doctrine to be unconsonant with several recitals, and one enactment in that grand act of Parliament, the petition of right in the 16th of Charles the First. He saw it also to be irreconcilable with the opinions declared by some of the greatest lawyers of that time to a committee of the whole House of Commons, sitting on martial law, namely, Sir Edward Cocke, Mr. Moy, afterwards Attorney-General, Mr. Rolle, afterwards Sergeant-at-Law, and author of the "Abridgment," Mr. Banks, afterwards successively Attorney-General and Lord Chief Justice of the Common Pleas, and Mr. Mason, distinguished both as a lawyer and a member of Parliament; for which opinions the author begs leave to refer to the preservation of them in the Appendix to Rushworth's third volume. Further, the author found such a latitude of martial law equally crossed by the doctrines of Lord Chief Justice Hale, as expressed in his manuscript and unprinted collections on the prerogative. This, the author trusts, will, without for the present looking further, sufficiently at least apologize for the strong terms used in those parts of his following opinion in the Grogan case which relate to martial law, even though volumes of cruel and irregular practice, during the sad extremities of civil war, should be laboriously collected, to overcome the potency of the petition of right; and of the high, grave, legal authorities, the author inclusively relies upon as speaking the same language."

[Here follows the opinion, but it is omitted, as not being necessary for the purposes of this discussion.]